In the
Small, Small Pond

For David, still the one.

ISBN 0-590-48119-3

Copyright © 1993 by Denise Fleming. All rights reserved. Published by Scholastic Inc., 555 Broadway, New York, NY 10012, by arrangement with Henry Holt and Company, Inc.

12 11 10 9 8 7 6 5 4 3 2   4 5 6 7 8 9/9

Printed in the U.S.A.   08

First Scholastic printing, September 1994

In the
Small, Small Pond

Denise Fleming

SCHOLASTIC INC.
New York Toronto London Auckland Sydney

In the small, small

pond...

tadpoles

wriggle

waddle,

wade,

geese parade

hover,

shiver,

wings quiver

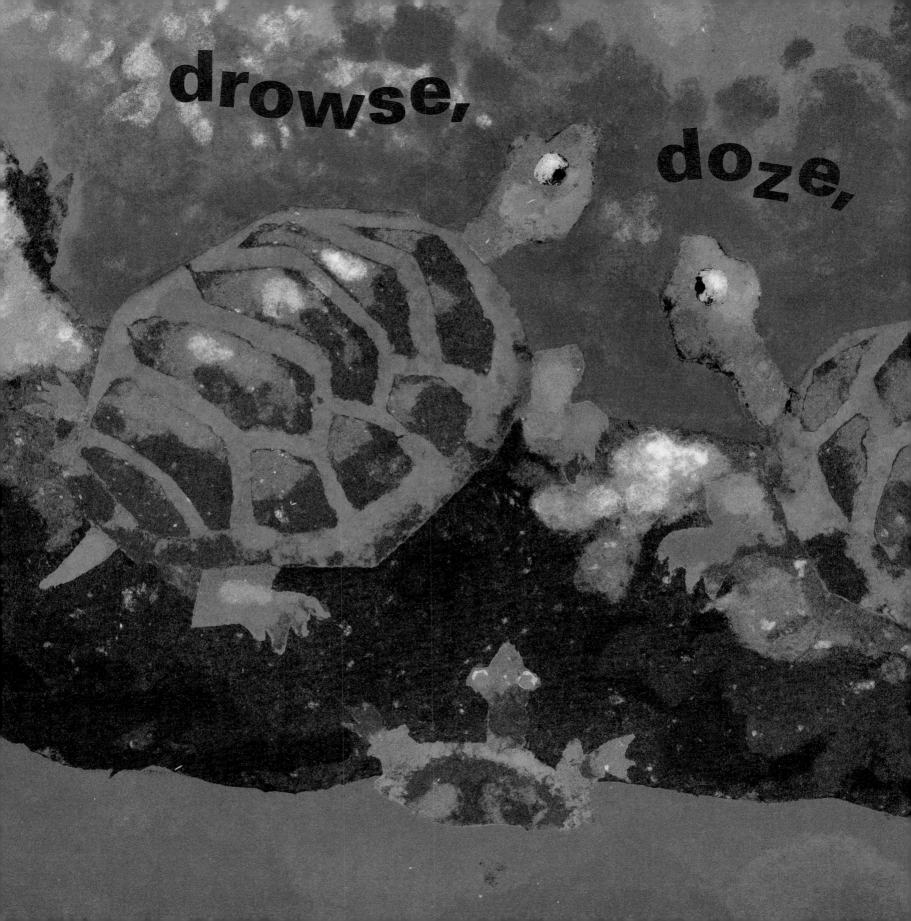

lash,

lunge,

herons

plunge

minnows scatter

circle, swirl,

whirligigs twirl

sweep, swoop,

swallows **scoop**

click, clack,

claws crack

dabble,

dip,

splish, splash, paws flash

pile,
pack,

muskrats
stack.

Chill breeze,

winter freeze...

cold night,

sleep tight,

small, small

pond.